Text copyright © Tony Bradman 2002
Illustrations copyright © Chris Hahner 2002
Book copyright © Hodder Wayland 2002

Consultant: Kim Reynolds, University of Surrey, Roehampton
Editor: Katie Orchard

Published in Great Britain in 2002
by Hodder Wayland, an imprint of
Hodder Children's Books

The right of Tony Bradman to be identified as the
author of this Work and of Chris Hahner as the
illustrator of this Work has been asserted by them in
accordance with the Copyright, Designs and Patents Act 1988.

Cataloguing in Publication Data
Bradman, Tony
A Christmas Carol – (Classic Collection)
1. Scrooge, Ebenezer (Ficticious character) – Juvenile fiction
2. England – Social life and customs
3. Christmas stories
4. Children's stories
I. Title II. Dickens, Charles, 1812–1870
823.9'14 [J]

ISBN: 0 7502 3667 1

Printed and bound in Hong Kong

Hodder Children's Books
A division of Hodder Headline Limited
338 Euston Road, London NW1 3BH

The Classic Collection

Charles Dickens'
A Christmas Carol

Retold by Tony Bradman
Illustrated by Chris Hahner

W
HODDER
Wayland

an imprint of Hodder Children's Books

An artist's impression of Charles Dickens,
1812–1870.

About Charles Dickens

Charles Dickens is one of the most famous writers of all time. He wrote many novels – among them *The Pickwick Papers, Oliver Twist, David Copperfield, Nicholas Nickleby, A Tale of Two Cities,* and *Great Expectations* – all of which were hugely successful during his life, and which are still read today.

He was born in Portsmouth in 1812, the second of eight brothers and sisters, and he died in 1870. During Charles' childhood, his father was put into prison for debt, and at the age of twelve Charles was sent to London to work in a factory to help support his family. It was a harsh experience, and one he never forgot.

Despite his lack of formal education, Charles became a reporter of debates in Parliament, and began to publish stories in his twenties. His first book, *The Pickwick Papers,* became a huge success. Most of his books were first published as serials, in magazines, and he gave a great number of public readings of them, too.

There was terrible poverty in Britain during the nineteenth century, and because of his childhood experiences, this was something that Dickens was deeply concerned about. His stories often feature characters struggling in the face of poverty, and he hoped that his books would help to change things.

He wrote *A Christmas Carol* in 1843, and in it he explores what greed can do to one man's life, and how it's never too late to change. The story could, in fact, be read as a plea for people to be more generous to each other, more aware of the suffering in the world, and less obsessed with themselves.

Charles Dickens enjoyed the Christmas season a great deal, and for him its message was the inspiration for *A Christmas Carol*. Perhaps that's why it's probably the most famous of all his stories, one that has been filmed many times, warning us all against greed. This much loved story has made Scrooge a household name.

Marley's Ghost

It was a bitterly cold, foggy Christmas Eve.
Ebenezer Scrooge sat at his desk, counting his
money. Oh! He was a tight-fisted hand at the
grindstone, Scrooge! A squeezing, wrenching,
grasping, scraping, clutching old man! It was
freezing in his poky little office, but Scrooge was
so mean he wouldn't let his clerk, Bob Cratchit,
put any coal on the tiny fire.

You could tell how mean Scrooge was from the sign outside his office. It still said: *Scrooge and Marley*, even though his partner, Jacob Marley, had died seven Christmases before. Scrooge wouldn't pay for it to be changed.

Suddenly the door flew open, and in came a cheerful young man. "Merry Christmas, Uncle!" he said. It was Fred, Scrooge's nephew.

"Bah, humbug!" Scrooge growled. "What use is Christmas to me? If I had my way, every idiot that goes about with 'Merry Christmas' on his lips would be boiled in his own pudding, and buried with a stake of holly through his heart!"

"You don't really mean that, Uncle!" said his nephew, smiling at him.

But Scrooge *did* mean it. He hated Christmas, and wanted nothing to do with it. He didn't want anything to do with his nephew, either, or his nephew's young wife. So Scrooge rudely turned down their invitation to dinner on Christmas Day.

Fred sighed, wished Bob Cratchit a *very* merry Christmas, and left.

There was to be no peace for old Scrooge, though. Two gentlemen came in next, seeking a donation to their charity fund for the poor.

"Are there no prisons or workhouses?" Scrooge said gruffly, sending the men away with nothing. "Let the poor go there – or they can die for all I care!"

Then a young carol singer came to the door and started singing. Scrooge seized a ruler from his desk and threatened the boy, who soon fled in terror.

When it was time to shut up the office for the
night, Scrooge turned to his clerk. "I suppose
you want all day off tomorrow?" he grumbled.

"If it's convenient, sir," said Bob Cratchit
hopefully. "It *is* only once a year…"

"Oh, very well," said Scrooge. "But you'd
better be here early the next day."

Bob Cratchit promised that he would, then
happily ran home to his wife and children.

Scrooge trudged homewards, came to his house at last, and went up the steps to his door. He put his key in the lock.

Suddenly, the door knocker changed into the face of his dead partner, Jacob Marley, then became a knocker again.

To say that Scrooge wasn't startled by this would be untrue. He was... But he turned the key in the lock, turned it sturdily, walked in and lit a candle. He did pause before he closed the door, and looked cautiously behind it, half expecting to see the back of Marley's head... but there was nothing there, and he said, "Bah!" then shut the door with a bang.

That evening, as Scrooge ate his lonely supper, he heard a terrible clanking. It drew nearer and nearer. Then a ghost walked through the closed door of Scrooge's chamber, dragging a huge, clanking chain behind it.

"I am the ghost of Jacob Marley," the phantom moaned. "And I have come to warn you, Ebenezer, and to help you escape my awful fate."

Marley had been mean and tight-fisted, just like Scrooge. Now he was doomed to eternal torment, carrying a heavy chain made of cash-boxes, purses and padlocks, the only things that had mattered to him in life.

He said that Scrooge would also wear such a chain in death, but his would be longer and much heavier. Unless Scrooge changed his ways, that is.

"Three more spirits will haunt you," said the ghost. "Without their visits you have no hope. Expect the first tomorrow when the clock strikes one. Expect the second at the same time on the following night. The third will come the night after that, on the last stroke of twelve."

"Couldn't I have them all at once, and get it over with?" asked Scrooge.

The ghost said nothing, but flew out of the window.

Tired and shaken, Scrooge went to bed, trying to forget what he'd seen. He fell instantly into a deep sleep…

The First of the Spirits

Scrooge was soon wide awake again. The clock
in the nearby church tower chimed quarter past
the hour, half past, quarter to, then…
ONE O'CLOCK!

Suddenly, Scrooge's bed curtains were drawn aside, and he found himself staring at a strange figure. It had the white hair of an old man, yet it had the face of a young child. It was wearing a white tunic decorated with summer flowers. A bright jet of light shone from its head. The figure held a cone-shaped cap.

"Are you the spirit I was told about?" Scrooge asked, shakily.

"Yes," breathed the spirit. "I am the Ghost of Christmas Past. *Your* past…"

Scrooge's fear was overwhelming and he barely felt the spirit's touch – a touch which transported them from Scrooge's familiar bedroom to a country road in cold daylight, with snow upon the ground.

"Good heavens!" said Scrooge. "I know this place. I was a boy here!"

They walked along the road and came to a school. Boys were leaving it, happy to be going home for Christmas. Scrooge recognized each one, but none acknowledged him.

"These shadows of the past can't see us," said the spirit. "But see, the school isn't quite deserted. A single child is left there, neglected by his friends."

They went into a room and Scrooge saw
himself, a lonely boy reading by a feeble fire.
Scrooge sobbed, and wished that he'd given
something to that poor carol singer he'd
chased away.

A young girl came running into the room.
"I'm here to bring you home, dear brother," she
said. It was Scrooge's little sister, Fan. "Father is
so much kinder than he used to be. He said you
could come home for Christmas, and you're
never to return to this place."

"A lovely, sweet girl who died young," said the spirit. "But she had a son."

"Yes, my nephew, Fred," said Scrooge, uneasily. "She *was* sweet and kind…"

Next the spirit took Scrooge back to a busy winter's evening in the city. Scrooge could tell from the decorations in the shops that it was Christmas.

They went into an office, where a plump, jolly man sat at a desk.

"Why, it's old Fezziwig!" said Scrooge. "I was an apprentice here!"

Then old Fezziwig called out to Scrooge's
former self – now grown into a young man –
and to Dick, another young apprentice Scrooge
recognized.

"Yo-ho, my boys!" laughed old Fezziwig. "No
more work for you tonight – it's Christmas Eve!
Let's get cracking. We need plenty of room
here!"

The two young men quickly cleared the furniture away. Mrs Fezziwig arrived, and the three Fezziwig daughters, and a fiddler, and lots more people. Soon the office was full of music, wild dancing and fun.

Scrooge stood unseen with the spirit, looking on, enjoying it all, listening to his former self and young Dick thanking Fezziwig over and over again for his kindness and generosity.

"You were easily pleased, weren't you?" said the spirit. "Fezziwig must have only spent a few pounds of his money on this party."

"There was more to it than money," said Scrooge. "He could have made our lives a misery, an endless toil. But he didn't. He made us happy…"

At that moment, Scrooge wished he could speak to Bob Cratchit.

But the spirit took him to another place.

Scrooge once again saw his former self, a little older now, and with a greedy, restless look, too. He was not alone, but sat beside a pretty young girl who was crying.

"You don't love me any more," she said. "We were both poor when we met but all you care about these days is money. If we were to meet for the first time now, you wouldn't be interested in me."

Scrooge's younger self tried to deny it, but his face gave him away. So he and the girl parted forever. The memory made Scrooge miserable.

But the spirit had something else to show him – Scrooge's love, happily married, surrounded by children.

Scrooge turned and looked at the spirit, and saw in its face all the faces it had shown him. It was too much for him to bear.

"Why are you torturing me, spirit?" demanded Scrooge. "Take me home!"

Scrooge angrily grabbed the spirit's cap and pulled it down over its head. But he couldn't stop the light streaming from underneath it. He felt exhausted and suddenly found himself in his own bed. Again he sank into a heavy sleep…

The Second of the Spirits

Scrooge woke in the middle of a huge snore, glad that he was awake before the next spirit arrived. He pulled back the curtains round his bed so that he would be ready to greet the spirit.

After a while he heard the clock strike one, but no spirit appeared, and Scrooge began to feel anxious. Five minutes, ten minutes, a quarter of an hour went by… Suddenly a warm blaze of light seemed to shine under the bedroom door. Scrooge got out of bed to see what it was.

The moment Scrooge's hand was on the doorknob, a strange voice called his name and told him to come in.

The room he entered was certainly his own room, but it had been completely transformed. It looked like a forest grove. The walls and ceiling were hung with fresh holly, mistletoe and ivy, and there was a huge, roaring blaze in the fireplace.

A wonderful heap of Christmas food was piled up on the floor, like a throne. And sitting on it was a jolly giant in a green robe, holding a torch.

"I am the Ghost of Christmas Present," said the giant, and he stood up.

"Spirit, take me where you will," said Scrooge, calmly.

The room vanished instantly, and Scrooge and the spirit were soon on the city streets. It was Christmas morning. The sky was gloomy and the streets were deep in snow and filled with fog. But everybody Scrooge saw seemed cheerful.

People threw snowballs, chattered happily as they queued at grocers' and bakers', and joyfully sang carols in church. Wherever Scrooge and the spirit went, the spirit sprinkled something from his torch that made the people merrier.

At last they came to a modest house and went inside. The spirit magically squeezed his giant form into a small room. The house was Bob Cratchit's, and Mrs Cratchit was getting things ready for the family's Christmas dinner.

Four of the Cratchit children were helping, then the fifth arrived from her work, and they wondered where their father was. He came at last, carrying on his shoulder his youngest child – poor, sickly Tiny Tim.

Together they ate their dinner – roast goose, eked out with apple-sauce and potatoes, followed by Christmas pudding, and there was just about enough for everybody. But they all thought it was a marvellous meal, just the same. The Cratchits weren't handsome, they weren't well dressed, and the family didn't have much money. But Scrooge could see that they were all happy.

"A merry Christmas to us all, my dears," said Bob. "God bless us!"

"God bless us, every one!" piped Tiny Tim. He sat close to his father, who held his hand tightly, as if he feared Tiny Tim might be taken from him.

"Spirit," said Scrooge, suddenly worried. "Tell me if Tiny Tim will live."

"I see an empty seat in the chimney corner," said the spirit. "If nothing happens to change the future, Tiny Tim will never see another Christmas."

"*No!*" cried Scrooge. "Say it isn't so! Say that he'll be spared."

"But why?" asked the spirit. "The poor can die for all you care…"

Scrooge bowed his head in shame, then lifted it when he heard his name.

Bob had raised his glass to give a Christmas toast to Mr Scrooge.

"I'd rather give that old skinflint a piece of my mind," said Mrs Cratchit. "But I'll drink his health for your sake, Bob, and because it's Christmas."

The children drank to Scrooge, too, but he could see that none of them liked the idea.

Soon Scrooge and the spirit were on their way again, flying through the darkening sky, watching people enjoying Christmas in homes everywhere.

And wherever the spirit took him, Scrooge could see that the people were happy, no matter how poor they were.

Suddenly Scrooge found himself in a room again. Somebody was laughing, and Scrooge saw that it was his nephew. The spirit was standing nearby, smiling.

"My uncle actually said that Christmas was humbug!" said Fred.

"I really don't know why you bother with him," said Fred's pretty young wife. There were others there, the couple's friends, and they agreed.

"I feel sorry for him, that's why," said Fred. "He's the one who always misses out on the fun everybody has at this time of year – and it would do him so much good. So I'll wish him 'Merry Christmas', whether he likes it or not!"

Everybody in the room laughed, and then there was music, and dancing, and games were played. And there was even a toast to Uncle Scrooge.

Old Scrooge loved to see the fun. He wanted to stay, but the spirit took him away once more.

The spirit was growing grey and old, and told Scrooge that its life would end at midnight.

They stopped in a cold, darkened street, chimes ringing out nearby. It was quarter to twelve… The spirit pulled back his robe to reveal two children it was sheltering, a boy and a girl, both of them ragged and ill and miserable.

"Are they yours, spirit?" asked Scrooge, stepping back, appalled.

"They belong to humanity," said the spirit. "One is Ignorance, the other, Want. Beware of both of them – but especially Ignorance."

"But don't they have anywhere to go?" said Scrooge. "A home, a refuge?"

"Are there no prisons or workhouses?" said the spirit as the clock struck twelve. The spirit and the children vanished, and Scrooge looked round.

A dark, hooded phantom was gliding steadily towards him.

The Last of the Spirits

The phantom approached Scrooge silently, and seemed to scatter gloom and mystery in the air through which it moved.

Scrooge knelt down before it. "Are you the Ghost of Christmas Yet To Come?" he asked.

The dark spirit said nothing, but pointed ahead.

"I fear you most of all," said Scrooge. "But since I know you are here to teach me, lead on…"

First, the spirit took Scrooge to the Exchange, where Scrooge did his business. A small group of men Scrooge knew stood talking. The spirit pointed at them, so Scrooge listened. It seemed that somebody had died.

"It will be a very cheap funeral," laughed one. "Nobody will come!"

Scrooge was puzzled, and looked around. But he couldn't see himself in the Exchange, and soon the spirit had whisked him off elsewhere.

They saw a dead man's things being sold to a rag and bone man, and a body lying dead on a bed, its face covered with a shroud. And they watched the Cratchits mourning poor Tiny Tim, who was no more, it seemed…

"Spirit," said Scrooge at last, "was I that man we saw lying dead?"

The spirit said nothing. But suddenly they were in a neglected graveyard, and the spirit was pointing at a grave. Scrooge trembled. He looked – and saw that the name on the headstone was… *EBENEZER SCROOGE!*

"Spirit!" Scrooge cried out, falling to his knees and grabbing at a ghostly hand. "Tell me that this is only what *might* happen. Tell me that if I change, the future won't be like this!'

Again, the spirit stayed silent, and tried to pull away its hand. But Scrooge held on, and cried out…

The End of It

Suddenly, Scrooge woke up, and found himself holding on to his own bedpost. He was so pleased to be alive, he leapt out of bed and danced all round the house. "I feel like a newborn baby!" he cried. "I'm going to make sure that things will be different from now on!"

Scrooge soon found out that the three spirits had done their work in a single night, and that it was the morning of Christmas Day. So he hadn't missed it, after all. Scrooge was determined to make amends straight away.

He had a splendid turkey sent to the Cratchits, and then he went to visit his nephew. On the way, Scrooge wished everyone he met a Merry Christmas, including one of the gentlemen who had come to his office on Christmas Eve. Scrooge promised him a handsome gift for his charity.

At last Scrooge came to Fred's house.

"It's me, Fred, your uncle Scrooge," he said. "Will you let me in?"

Fred was delighted to see him, and so was Fred's wife when she saw how happy and hearty Scrooge was. They had a wonderful, happy Christmas day.

The next day at his office, Scrooge told Bob to put more coal on the fire – and then he raised his wages!

Scrooge enjoyed many happy Christmases, and became a second father to Tiny Tim, who *did* live, and grew healthy. So, as Tiny Tim said – "God bless us, every one!"

The Classic Collection

Look out for these other titles in *The Classic Collection*:

Jane Eyre Retold by Belinda Hollyer
Jane Eyre longs for love and friendship. She believes she has
found it when she meets the dashing Mr Rochester. But his
mysterious behaviour hides a dark secret – can their love
survive it? A passionate retelling of a love story that has
captivated readers for over 150 years.

Gulliver's Travels Retold by Beverley Birch
Gulliver is shipwrecked and washed ashore on the exotic island
of Lilliput – where the people are only six inches tall! This is
just the start of Gulliver's unbelievable adventure. A thrilling
retelling of one of the most exciting fantasy stories ever written.

The Pardoner's Tale Retold by Jan Dean
On a trip to Canterbury, the crooked Pardoner tells a crooked
story about a gang of youths who decide to hunt down Death
and kill him. Little do they know that Death will find them
first! A lively retelling of a story that is as hilarious today as
when it was written over six centuries ago.

You can buy all these books from your local bookseller, or
order them direct from the publisher. For more information
about *The Classic Collection*, write to: *The Sales Department,
Hodder Children's Books, a division of Hodder Headline Limited,
338 Euston Road, London NW1 3BH.*